10 Little PENGuiNS

KaTe ToMs

Castle Street PRESS

10

little penguins are

but 1 of them has lost her

Where's Pamela?

playful penguins are

9

bouncing really high . . . .

1 penguin
jumps too far
and zooms up
to the sky!

dressed-up penguins

8

are looking really happy . . .

but 1 of them is way too warm.

I'm off!

It makes him rather snappy.

busy penguins each

1 penguin eats
too fast and now
has tummy ache!

Oh dear!

happy penguins, all singing

6

playing with their toys....

1 of them decides to leave; she doesn't like the noise.

5 quiet penguins watch

but 1 has seen this one before

and thinks it's time to go.

their favorite show . . .

4 hungry penguins are

1 dries, "Not sardines!" and jumps

sitting down to eat....
up from his seat!

funny penguins are

3

Skating 'round and 'round and 'round...

Keep it smooooooth!

and crashes

to the ground!

a somersault

1 tries

smelly penguins take

2

Tee hee Tee hee

a bubble bath ....

1 slips on
a bar of soap,
and makes
the other laugh!

tired little penguin.

1

She thought her friends

But look!
They're in her bed!

had all gone home . . .

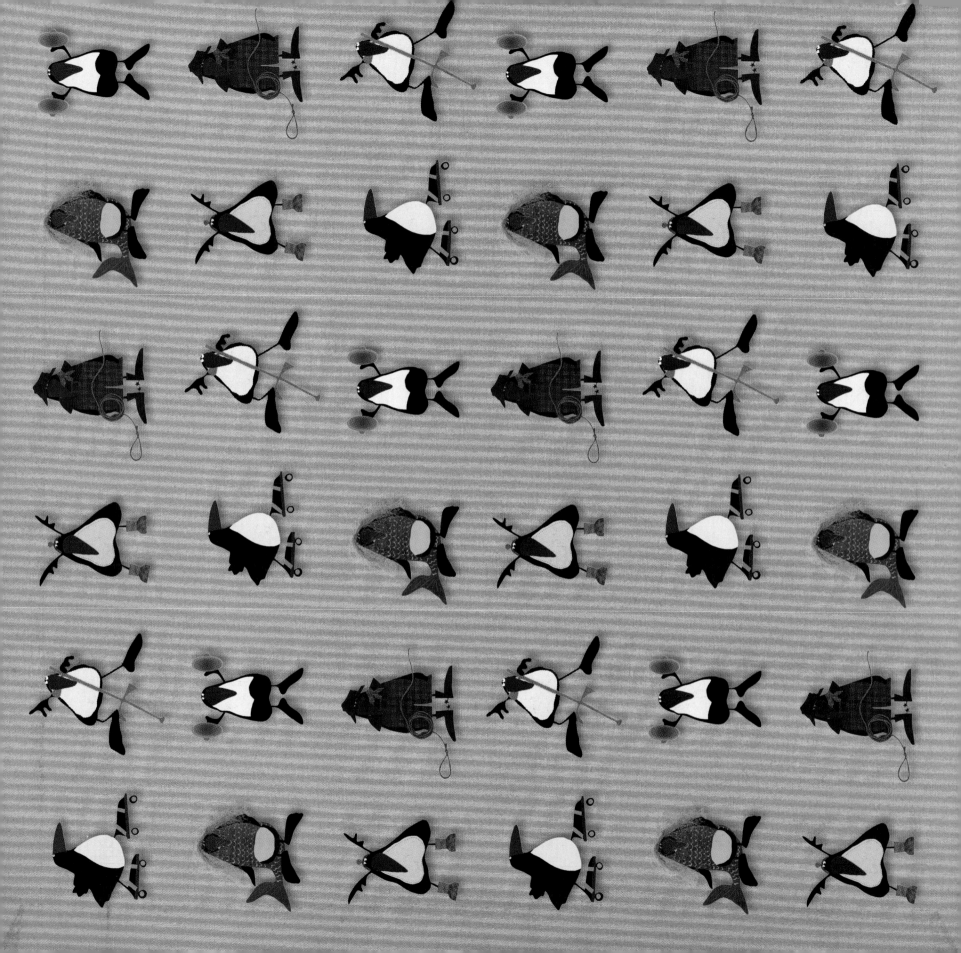